22.4.23

19|8|23

Please renew or return items by the date
shown on your receipt

www.hertfordshire.gov.uk/libraries

Renewals and enquiries: 0300 123 4049

Textphone for hearing or 0300 123 4041
speech impaired users:

L32 11.16

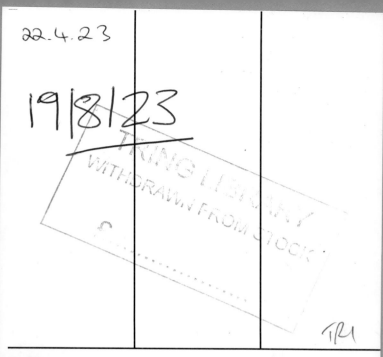

D1439482

530 131 35 6

HORRiD HENRY'S
Newspaper

HORRiD HENRY'S
Newspaper

Francesca Simon
Illustrated by Tony Ross

Orion
Children's Books

Horrid Henry's Newspaper **was originally published in** *Horrid Henry Robs the Bank*, **but appears here for the first time in a single volume with brand-new full-colour illustrations.**

ORION CHILDREN'S BOOKS

Horrid Henry's Newpaper first appeared in *Horrid Henry Robs the Bank*
First published in Great Britain in 2008 by Orion Children's Books
This Early Reader edition first published in Great Britain in 2020
by Hodder and Stoughton

1 3 5 7 9 10 8 6 4 2

Text © Francesca Simon, 2008
Illustrations © Tony Ross, 2008

The rights of Francesca Simon and Tony Ross to be identified as author and
illustrator of this work have been asserted.

A CIP catalogue record for this book is available from the British Library.

ISBN 978 1 5101 0624 6

Printed and bound in China

The paper and board used in this book are from well-managed forests and other
responsible sources.

Orion Children's Books
An imprint of
Hachette Children's Group
Part of Hodder & Stoughton
Carmelite House
50 Victoria Embankment
London EC4Y 0DZ

An Hachette UK Company
www.hachette.co.uk
www.hachettechildrens.co.uk
www.horridhenry.co.uk

*For my brilliant friend
Dina Rabinovitch*

Look out for:

Don't Be Horrid, Henry!
Horrid Henry's Birthday Party
Horrid Henry's Holiday
Horrid Henry's Underpants
Horrid Henry Gets Rich Quick
Horrid Henry and the Football Fiend
Horrid Henry's Nits
Horrid Henry and Moody Margaret
Horrid Henry's Thank You Letter
Horrid Henry and the School Fair
Horrid Henry and the Zombie Vampire
Horrid Henry's Hike

There are many more Early Reader
titles available.

For a complete list visit horridhenry.co.uk

Contents

Chapter 1

"It's not fair!" howled Horrid Henry. "I want a Hip-Hop Robot dog!" Horrid Henry needed money. Lots and lots and lots of money.

His parents didn't need money, and yet they had loads more than he did. It was so unfair.

Why was he so brilliant at spending
money, and so bad at getting money?
And now Mum and Dad refused
to buy him something he
desperately needed.

"You have plenty of toys," said Mum.
"Which you never play with,"
said Dad.

"That's 'cause they're all so boring!"
screeched Henry. "I want a
robot dog!"
"Too expensive," said Mum.
"Too noisy," said Dad.
"But everyone has a Hip-Hop Robot
Dog," whined Henry. "Everyone
but me."

Horrid Henry stomped out of the room. How could he get some money? Wait. Maybe he could persuade Peter to give him some. Peter always had tons of cash because he never bought anything.

Yes! He could hold Peter's Bunnykins
for ransom. He could tell Peter his
room was haunted and get Peter
to pay him for ghostbusting. He
could make Peter donate to Henry's
favourite charity, Child in Need . . .
Hip-Hop Robot Dog, here I come,
thought Horrid Henry, bursting into
Peter's bedroom.

Perfect Peter and Tidy Ted were
whispering together on the floor.
Papers were scattered all
around them.
"You can't come in my room,"
said Peter.

"Yes I can," said Henry, "'cause I'm already in. Pooh, your room stinks." "That's 'cause you're in it," said Peter. Henry decided to ignore this insult. "Whatcha doing?"

"Nothing," said Peter.
"We're writing our own newspaper
like Mrs Oddbod suggested in
assembly," said Ted. "We've even got
a 'Tidy with Ted' column,"
he added proudly.

"A snooze paper, you mean,"
said Henry.
"It is not," said Peter.
Henry snorted. "What's it called?"
"*The Best Boys' Busy Bee*,"
said Peter.

"What a stupid name," said Henry.
"It's not a stupid name," said Peter.
"Miss Lovely said it was perfect."
"Peter, I have a great idea for your
paper," said Henry.

"What?" said Peter cautiously.
"You can use your newspaper for
Fluffy's cat litter tray."

"MUUUM!" wailed Peter. "Henry's being mean to me."
"Don't be horrid, Henry!" shouted Mum.

Chapter 2

"Peter is a poopsicle, Peter is a
poopsicle," chanted Henry.
But then Peter did something strange.
Instead of screaming for Mum,
Peter started writing.

"Now everyone who buys my newspaper will know how horrid you are," said Peter, putting down his pencil.

Buy? Buy?

"We're selling it in school tomorrow,"
said Ted. "Miss Lovely said we could."

Sell? Sell?

"Lemme see that," said
Henry, yanking the paper
out of Peter's hands.
The Busy Bee's headline read:

PETER IN THE GOOD AS GOLD BOOK FOR THE FOURTH TIME THIS MONTH

Horrid Henry snorted.
What a worm.

Then his eye caught the second
headline:

COMPUTER BAN FOR
HORRID BOY

Henry was banned from playing games
on the computer today because he was
mean to his brother Peter and called him
wibble pants and poopsicle. *The Busy Bee*
hopes Henry has learned his lesson and
will stop being such a big meanie.

"You're going to . . . sell this?"
spluttered Henry. His name would be
mud. Worse than mud. Everyone
would know what a stupid toad
brother he had. Worse, some people
might even believe Peter's lies.

And then suddenly Horrid Henry had a brilliant, spectacular idea. He'd write his own newspaper. Everyone would want to buy it. He'd be rich!

He could call his newspaper *The Hourly Howler* and charge 25p a copy. If he could write seven editions a day, and sell each copy to 500 people, he'd make . . . he'd make . . . well, multiplication was never his best subject, but he could make tons of money!!!!!!

On the other hand, writing seven
newspapers a day, every day, seemed
an awful lot of work. An awful, awful
lot of work. Perhaps *The Daily Digger*
was the way to go. He'd charge a lot
more per copy, and do a lot
less work. Yes!

Hmmn. Perhaps *The Weekly Warble* would be better. No, *The Monthly Moaner*. Maybe just *The Purple Hand Basher*.

The Basher! What a great name for a great paper!

Now, what should his
newspaper have?
News of course. All about
Henry's triumphs. And gossip and
quizzes and sport.

Chapter 3

First, I need a great headline, thought
Horrid Henry. What about:
PETER IS A WORM.
Tempting, thought Henry, but old
news: everyone already knows that
Peter is a worm.

What could he tell his readers that
they didn't know? After all, news
didn't have to be true, did it?
Just new. And boy did he have
some brand-new news!

PETER SENT TO PRISON

The world's toadiest brother has been found guilty of being a worm and taken straight to prison. He was sentenced to live on bread and water for three years. *The Basher* says: "It should have been ten years."

SECRET CLUB
COLLAPSES!!!

The Secret Club has collapsed.

"Margaret is such a moody old bossy-boots no one wants to be in her club any more," said Susan.

"Goodbye, grump-face," said Gurinder.

Right, that was the news section taken care of. Now, for some good gossip. But what gossip? What scandal? Sadly, Horrid Henry didn't know any horrid rumours. But a gossip columnist needed to write something . . .

MRS ODDBOD BIKINI SHOCK

Mrs Oddbod was seen strolling down the High Street wearing a new yellow polka dot bikini. Is this any way for a head teacher to behave?

TEACHER IN
TOILET TERROR

Terrible screams rang out from the boys' toilets yesterday. "Help! Help! There's a monster in the loo!" screamed the crazed teacher Miss Boudicca Battle-Axe. "It's got hairy scary claws and three heads!!"

GUESS WHO?

Which soggy swimming teacher was seen dancing the cha-cha-cha with which old battle-axe?

MISS LOVELY IN NOSE PICK HORROR

Oh dear, Miss Lydia Lovely picks her nose.

"I saw her do it in class," says Prisoner Peter. "But she said it was her nose and she would pick it if she wanted to."

NIT NURSE HAS NITS!

Nitty Nora, Bug Explorer was sent home from school with nits last week. Whoopee! No more bug-busting!

That's enough great gossip for one
issue, thought Horrid Henry. Now,
what else, what else? A bit about
sports and he was done.
In tomorrow's edition, he'd add
a comic strip: The adventures of
Peter the Nappy.
And a quiz:

Who has the smelliest pants in
school?
A. Peter
B. Margaret
C. Susan
D. All of the above!

Yippee! thought Horrid Henry. I'm going to be rich, rich, rich, rich, rich.

The next morning, Henry made sure he got to school bright and early. Hip-hop Robot, here I come, thought Horrid Henry, lugging a huge pile of *Bashers* into the playground. Then he stopped.

A terrible sight met his eyes.
Moody Margaret and Sour Susan
were standing in the school
playground waving big
sheets of paper.

"Step right up, read all about it,
Margaret made Captain of the school
football team," bellowed Moody
Margaret. "Get your *Daily Dagger*
right here. Only 25p!"

Chapter 4

What a copycat, thought
Horrid Henry. He was outraged.
"Who'd want to read that?" sneered
Horrid Henry.

"Everyone," said Susan.
Horrid Henry snatched a copy.
"That'll be 25p, Henry,"
said Margaret.
Henry ignored her.

The headline read:

MARGARET TRIUMPHS

Margaret, the best footballer in school history, beat out her puny opposition to become captain of the school football team! Well done Margaret! Everyone cheered for hours when Mrs Oddbod announced the glorious news.

Margaret gave an exclusive interview to the **Daily Dagger**:

"It's hard being as amazing as I am," said Margaret. "So many people are jealous, especially pongy pants pimples like Henry."

"What a load of rubbish," said
Horrid Henry, scrunching up
Margaret's newspaper.

"Our customers don't think so,"
said Margaret. "I'm making loads
of loot. Before you know it I'll
have the first Hip-Hop Robot Dog.
And you-ooooo won't," she chanted.

"We'll see about that," said Horrid
Henry. "Teacher in toilet terror! Read
all about it!" he hollered. "All the
news and gossip. Only 25p."

"News! News!" screeched Margaret.
"Step right up, step right up!
Only 24p."

"Buy the *Busy Bee*!" piped Peter.
"Only 5p."

Rude Ralph bought a *Basher*. So did
Dizzy Dave and Jolly Josh.

Lazy Linda approached
Margaret.
"Oy, Linda, don't buy that
rubbish," shouted Henry. "I've
got the best news and gossip."

Henry whispered in Linda's ear.
Her jaw dropped and she handed
Henry 25p.

Chapter 5

"Don't listen to him!" squealed
Margaret.

"Buy the *Busy Bee*," trilled Perfect Peter. "Free vegetable chart."

"Margaret, did you see what Henry wrote about you?" gasped Gorgeous Gurinder.

"What?" said Margaret, grabbing a *Basher*.

SPORTS
SHOCK FOOTBALL NEWS

There was shock all round when Henry wasn't made captain of the school football team.

"It's an outrage," said Dave.

"Disgusting," said Soraya.

The Basher was lucky enough to get an exclusive interview with Henry.

"Not making me captain just goes to show what an idiot that old carrot-nose Miss Battle-Axe is," says Henry.

The Basher says: **Make Henry captain!**

"What!" screamed Margaret. "Dave and Soraya never said that."
"They thought it," said Henry. He glared at Moody Margaret. Moody Margaret glared at Horrid Henry. Henry's hand reached out to pull Margaret's hair. Margaret's foot reached out to kick Henry's leg.

Suddenly Mrs Oddbod walked into the playground. There was a stern-looking man with her, wearing a suit and carrying a notebook. Miss Battle-Axe and Miss Lovely followed.

Chapter 6

Aha, new customers, thought Horrid
Henry, as they headed towards him.
"Get your school paper here!"
hollered Henry. "Only 50p."
"News! News!" screeched Margaret.

"Step right up, step right up! 49p."
"Buy the *Busy Bee*!" trilled Peter.
"Only 5p."
"Well, well," said the strange man.
"What have we here, Mrs Oddbod?"

Mrs Oddbod beamed. "Just three of our best students showing how enterprising they are," she said.

Horrid Henry thought his ears had
fallen off. Best student? And why was
Mrs Oddbod smiling at him?
Mrs Oddbod never smiled at him.

"Peter, why don't you tell the
inspector what you're doing,"
said Miss Lovely.

"I've written my own newspaper
to raise money for the school," said
Perfect Peter.

"Very impressive, Mrs Oddbod," said
the school inspector, smiling.
"Very impressive. And what about
you, young man?" he added,
turning to Henry.

"I'm selling my newspaper for a
Child in Need," said Horrid Henry.
In need of a Hip-Hop Robot,
he thought.
"How many do you want to buy?"

The school inspector handed over
50p and took a paper.
"I love school newspapers," he said,
starting to read. "You find out so
much about what's really happening
at a school."
The school inspector gasped. Then he
turned to Mrs Oddbod.

"What do you know about a yellow polka dot bikini?" said the Inspector. "Yellow . . . polka . . . dot . . . bikini?" said Mrs Oddbod.

"Cha-cha-cha?" choked Miss Battle-Axe.

"Nose-picking?" gasped Miss Lovely.

★★★

"But what's the point of writing
news that everyone knows?"
protested Horrid Henry afterwards
in Mrs Oddbod's office.
"News should be new."

Just wait till tomorrow's edition . . .

Read all the Horrid Henry Early Readers:

Early Reader

HORRID HENRY'S
Haunted
House

Francesca Simon
Illustrated by Tony Ross

Early Reader

HORRID HENRY'S
Christmas
Lunch

Francesca Simon
Illustrated by Tony Ross

Early Reader

HORRID HENRY'S
Mother's
Day

Francesca Simon
Illustrated by Tony Ross

Early Reader

HORRID HENRY'S
Holiday

Francesca Simon
Illustrated by Tony Ross

Early Reader

HORRID HENRY'S
Christmas
Lunch

Francesca Simon
Illustrated by Tony Ross

Early Reader

HORRID HENRY
Tricks the
Tooth
Fairy

Francesca Simon
Illustrated by Tony Ross

Early Reader

HORRID HENRY
Gets Rich
Quick

Francesca Simon
Illustrated by Tony Ross

Early Reader

HORRID HENRY'S
Rainy Day

Illustrated by
Tony Ross

Francesca Simon

Early Reader

HORRID HENRY
and the Fangmangler

Francesca Simon
Illustrated by Tony Ross

Early Reader

HORRID HENRY'S
Christmas
Ambush

Francesca Simon
Illustrated by Tony Ross

Early Reader

HORRID HENRY'S
Swimming Lesson

Francesca Simon
Illustrated by Tony Ross

Early Reader

HORRID HENRY'S
School Fair

Francesca Simon
Illustrated by Tony Ross

Early Reader

ORRID HENRY'S
Hike

Francesca Simon
Illustrated by Tony Ross

Early Reader

HORRID HENRY'S
Injection

Francesca Simon
Illustrated by Tony Ross

Early Reader

HORRID HENRY'S
NIGHTMARE

FRANCESCA SIMON
ILLUSTRATED BY TONY ROSS

Early Reader

HORRID HENRY'S
NEWSPAPER

FRANCESCA SIMON
ILLUSTRATED BY TONY ROSS

Learn to read with Horrid Henry!